The Everglades: Analyzing
Graphs, Tables, and Charts
Colleen Adams
AR B.L.: 7.9
Points: 1.0

The Everglades

Analyzing Graphs, Tables, and Charts

Colleen Adams

PowerMath™

The Rosen Publishing Group's
PowerKids Press™
New York

Published in 2005 by The Rosen Publishing Group, Inc.
29 East 21st Street, New York, NY 10010

Book Design: Michael J. Flynn

Photo Credits: Cover, p. 23 © David Muench/Corbis; pp. 8, 12 © Patrick Ward/Corbis; p. 11 ©
Jim Sugar/Corbis; p. 15 © Dave G. Houser/Corbis; p. 17 © Darrell Gulin/Corbis; p. 19 (crocodile) ©
Martin B. Withers; Frank Lane Picture Agency/Corbis; p. 19 (Florida panther) © Kennan Ward/Corbis;
p. 20 © Amos Nachoum/Corbis; p. 25 © Tony Arruza/Corbis.

Library of Congress Cataloging-in-Publication Data

Adams, Colleen.
  The Everglades : analyzing graphs, tables, and charts / Colleen Adams.
      p. cm. — (PowerMath)
  Includes bibliographical references and index.
  ISBN 1-4042-2933-7 (lib. bdg.)
  ISBN 1-4042-5127-8 (pbk.)
  6-pack ISBN 1-4042-5128-6
  1. Graphic methods—Juvenile literature. 2. Statistics—Juvenile literature. 3. Everglades (Fla.)—Juvenile
literature. I. Title. II. Series.
  QA90.A28 2005
  001.4'226—dc22
                                    2004005315

Manufactured in the United States of America

Contents

Using Data to Understand the Everglades

We can use charts, tables, and graphs to learn more about the climate, wildlife, plants, and **habitats** of the Everglades, a unique **ecosystem** in southern Florida. A chart is a group of facts about a topic that is arranged in the form of a diagram, table, or graph. A table organizes data into columns and rows so that it is easy to read.

A graph displays data or charts changes in one or more things using lines, dots, bars, or parts of a circle. Line graphs and bar graphs show changes over time. Double line graphs and double bar graphs are used to compare 2 or more sets of data. Circle graphs—also known as pie charts—are used to represent a part-to-whole relationship.

Tables, graphs, and charts can help you compare facts and figures about topics related to the Everglades and draw conclusions about this information. For example, a bar graph can be used to show the difference between the average rainfall in the Everglades during the wet season and the average rainfall during the dry season. A line graph can be used to show the decline of the wood stork population in the Everglades over a period of years. A table can be used to compare the number of people who visited the Everglades in specific years. You can use these tables, graphs, and charts to help you organize information, make comparisons, and analyze data quickly.

Page 5 shows 2 graphs, a chart, and a table that you will see later on in this book. How are the graphs, the chart, and the table different? How are they the same?

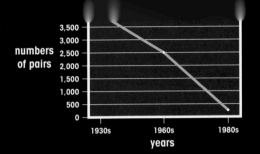

numbers of pairs

3,500
3,000
2,500
2,000
1,500
1,000
500
0

1930s   1960s   1980s

years

pie chart

food habits of the Florida panther

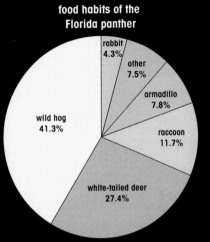

rabbit 4.3%

other 7.5%

armadillo 7.8%

raccoon 11.7%

wild hog 41.3%

white-tailed deer 27.4%

bar graph

average monthly rainfall in the Everglades

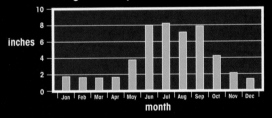

inches

10
8
6
4
2
0

Jan Feb Mar Apr May Jun Jul Aug Sep Oct Nov Dec

month

table

annual number of visitors to Everglades National Park

year	visitors
1948	7,482
1958	433,255
1968	1,251,453
1972	1,773,302
1978	1,136,177
1988	1,071,372
1998	1,177,477

The Everglades ecosystem is the only one of its kind in the United States. Its location in southern Florida between **temperate** and tropical zones makes it possible for many kinds of animals to live in its many different habitats. The large variety of animals that live there include **invertebrates**, both freshwater and saltwater fish, amphibians, reptiles, mammals, and birds. The damp climate is home to many plants that cannot be found anywhere else in the world. Much of this region is now included in Everglades National Park.

For thousands of years, water flowing from the Kissimmee River into Lake Okeechobee spread out over the low, flat grassland to the south, turning this area into a large wetland. The freshwater moved slowly over the lowlands, which were covered by thick **saw grass**. The Everglades region is sometimes called the "river of grass" due to the large amount of saw grass that grows in the shallow water. The highest elevation in the Everglades is only about 10 feet above sea level. This causes large areas of land to become partially or totally covered in water. Over time, the land of the Everglades formed the shape of a shallow basin that tilts slightly from Lake Okeechobee to the Gulf of Mexico.

In 1947, President Truman established 460,000 acres of land in southern Florida as Everglades National Park. The park's size has been increased 3 times since then, most recently in 1989, when the Everglades National Park Protection and Expansion Act added 109,000 acres. This line graph shows the expansion of Everglades National Park from 1947 to 1989.

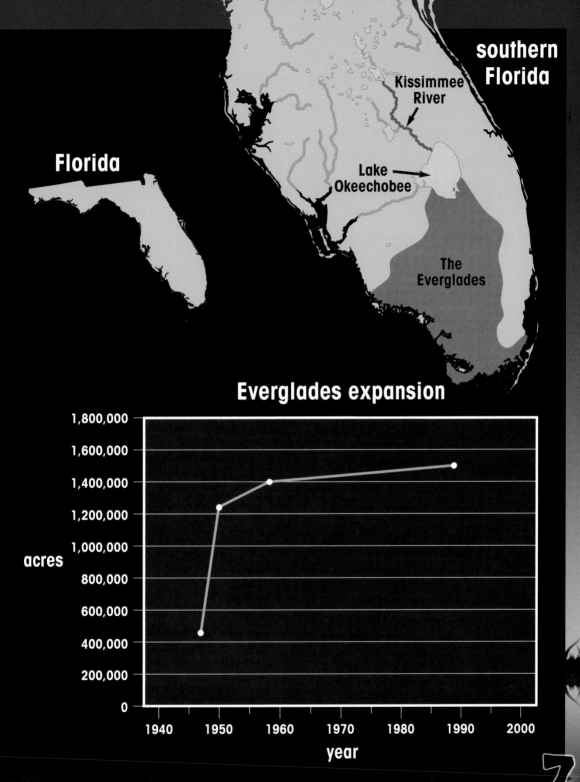

Florida

southern Florida

Kissimmee River

Lake Okeechobee

The Everglades

Everglades expansion

acres

year

7

Everglades National Park—which makes up approximately $\frac{1}{5}$ of the Everglades region—is the largest **subtropical** wilderness area in the United States. It was established in 1947 to protect the plants and wildlife occupying the Everglades region. The varied habitats in Everglades National Park include grasslands, forests, saltwater and freshwater marshes, and bays. There are more than 350 kinds of birds, 50 kinds of reptiles, and 40 kinds of mammals that live on this **preserve**. The hundreds of different flowers that grow in the Everglades include ferns, orchids, **bromeliads**, and water lilies.

Some visitors to the park, like those shown below, come to see the 14 **endangered** and 8 **threatened** wildlife species in the Everglades. Endangered animals such as the Florida panther, the West Indian manatee, and the wood stork are watched carefully and protected by environmental groups. The wood stork is an "indicator species" for the Everglades. This means that the wood stork's survival requirements are closely related to the Everglades habitat. When the characteristics of the Everglades change, the habitat can no longer sustain wood storks as it once did. When the wood stork population of the Everglades declines, this "indicates" that the Everglades ecosystem is in danger. When the wood stork population increases, this "indicates" that conditions in the Everglades are improving.

year	visitors
1948	7,482
1958	433,255
1968	1,251,453
1972	1,773,302
1978	1,136,177
1988	1,071,372
1998	1,177,477

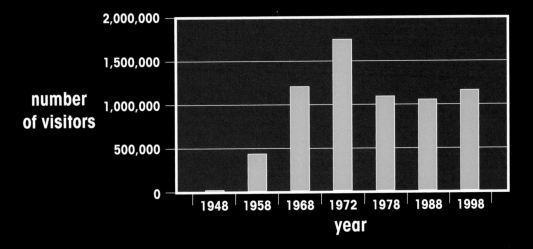

This table and bar graph show the number of visitors to the Everglades in 10-year increments. The number of visitors for 1972 has been included because that was the year when the most people visited the Everglades. In what year did the fewest people visit?

The Habitats of the Everglades

In the Everglades there are wet and dry seasons, freshwater and saltwater areas, temperate and tropical zones, different elevations of land, and different types of soil. These features make it possible for a wide variety of plants and animals to live there. Animals such as black bears, bobcats, and white-tailed deer live in the forests. Alligators, crocodiles, turtles, manatees, snakes, and otters live in the marshes and waterways. Many kinds of wading birds—such as herons, egrets, and spoonbills—often nest and feed here as well. Trout, dolphins, and sharks are just a few of the animals that live in the area's bays.

Freshwater marshes include saw grass marshes, which cover large areas of land from Lake Okeechobee to the Gulf of Mexico. The saw grass, cattails, **sedges**, and grasses that grow here absorb some of the water flow on its way to the Gulf of Mexico. This process creates soil conditions that provide ideal homes for many kinds of wildlife. Algae that grow in freshwater marshes during the dry season are the beginning of a food chain that supplies food for birds, fish, mammals, amphibians, and reptiles.

This bar graph shows the average monthly rainfall in southern Florida during a year. The highest monthly rainfalls occur between May and October, which is called the wet season. Which month shows the highest rainfall?

marshland

average monthly rainfall in the Everglades

inches vs. month

Forests of red, white, and black mangrove trees are found along the coast and flooded saltwater areas at the southern tip of Florida. Freshwater from Lake Okeechobee mixes with salt water from the Gulf of Mexico to form **estuaries** that provide an ideal **environment** for many kinds of land and water animals. This habitat provides feeding and nesting places for many kinds of wading birds, turtles, manatees, and crocodiles, and a home for shrimp and fish. The Everglades estuaries are made up of saltwater marshes, mangrove forests, and Florida Bay. The leaves, branches, and trunks of mangrove trees eventually decay and fall into the water, providing food for the animals that live in this habitat.

mangroves

Florida Bay is the largest body of water within Everglades National Park. Located between the southern tip of Florida and a long row of islands called the Florida Keys, it covers over 850 square miles. More than 700 square miles of the bay are within the boundaries of Everglades National Park. The bottom of the bay has a coral reef habitat that is home to many marine animals, including over 100 different kinds of fish. Mangrove forests grow along the shores of the bay.

habitats of the Everglades

habitat	habitat characteristics
hardwood hammocks	Forests of hardwood trees that grow in tropical and temperate climates.
Florida Bay	The largest body of water in the Everglades, which has a coral reef and provides food for many marine animals.
mangrove forests	Forests of red, white, and black mangrove trees that grow in saltwater areas.
cypress domes	Forests of cypress trees that grow in a circular pattern in standing water.
pinelands	Forests of many slash pine trees, palms, palmettos, and wildflowers.
saltwater marshes	Areas along the coast where freshwater and salt water meet.
freshwater marshes	Shallow wetlands with standing water that lasts most of the year. Saw grass and other plants grow here.

This table shows characteristics of the different habitats that exist in the Everglades. How many kinds of forests are in the Everglades?

13

Hammocks are slightly elevated sections of land called tree islands. Over 150 kinds of tropical plants, including trees and shrubs, grow on the hammocks. Trees that thrive in temperate climates—such as willows, dahoon hollies, red bays, and red maples—can be found on the hardwood hammocks. Tropical trees such as the mahogany, gumbo limbo, and coco plum can also be found in the Everglades. Many kinds of wildlife can be found in the hammocks, including birds, snakes, lizards, tree frogs, bobcats, and deer.

Cypress trees are found in several different areas in the Everglades. These trees grow close together and can live in standing water. In some areas called cypress domes, the trees grow in a circular pattern. Trees in the center grow taller than those on the outer edges. Bromeliads, orchids, and other **epiphytes** (EH-puh-fyts), or air plants, grow on the bark of the cypress trees. The roots of the trees have "knees" that poke out above the soil near the base of the tree. Many kinds of amphibians, reptiles, mammals, and birds can be found in this freshwater area.

The pinelands, or pine flatwood forests, grow mainly in a sandy area of the eastern Everglades. The slash pine is very common in the pinelands. Sable palms, palmettos, shrubs, and a variety of wildflowers also grow here. Birds, deer, squirrels, bobcats, skunks, snakes, and tortoises are commonly found in the pinelands.

The chart and table at the top of page 15 represent a section of the hardwood hammocks of the Everglades.

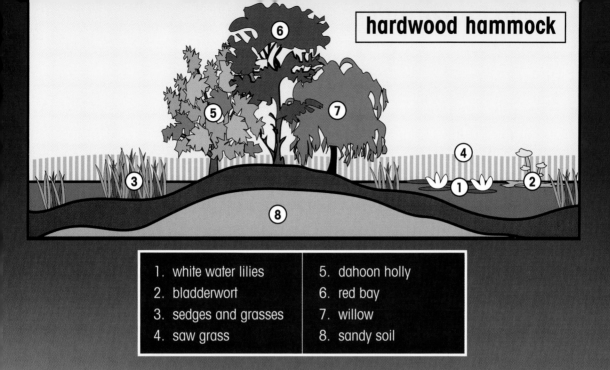

hardwood hammock

1. white water lilies	5. dahoon holly
2. bladderwort	6. red bay
3. sedges and grasses	7. willow
4. saw grass	8. sandy soil

Endangered Animals

Several animals that live in the Everglades are considered threatened or endangered. Endangered animals are animals in danger of becoming extinct due to changes in their environment. Threatened wildlife will become endangered if steps are not taken to protect their populations and their natural habitats. Overdevelopment of natural areas, pollution, drainage of water through canals and dams, and redirection of the water flow out of the Everglades have caused considerable damage and loss to many animal habitats in the region. The water-control systems used to take water in and out of the Everglades have changed the natural cycle of the wet and dry seasons. This affects the ability of some animals, particularly the wood stork, to find food and build nests.

For many years, Everglades National Park has provided a safe place for many kinds of wading birds that depend on the yearly dry-and-wet cycle for food, water, and mating. The dry season lasts from December to April. During the dry season, water levels slowly drop. Wading birds like the egret, spoonbill, and heron gather in shallow freshwater areas to eat fish. When there is not enough water, there are not enough fish for the birds to eat. This, in turn, affects the feeding and mating habits of the wading birds and other animals.

The line graph at the top of page 17 shows the large decline in the wood stork population in the Everglades between the 1930s and today. The wood stork has been on the endangered list since 1984.

16

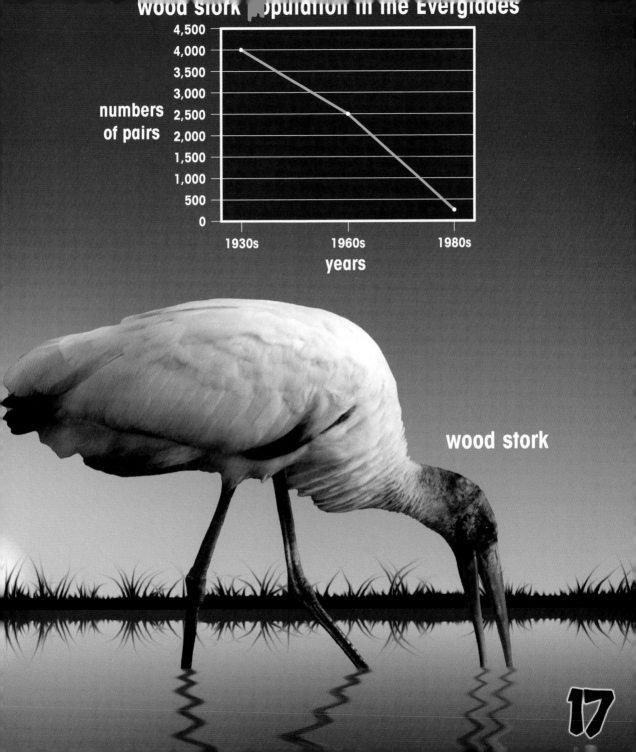

Wood Stork Population in the Everglades

numbers
of pairs

4,500
4,000
3,500
3,000
2,500
2,000
1,500
1,000
500
0

1930s   1960s   1980s

years

wood stork

17

The American crocodile is a reptile that can grow to be 15 feet in length or longer. The crocodile is about the same size as an alligator, but has a narrower snout and is a lighter color. Crocodiles are sometimes seen in coastal mangrove swamps and in Florida Bay. With the construction of dams to supply water to homes and farms outside of the Everglades, the amount of salt in Florida Bay is rising. Adult crocodiles can adapt to saltwater conditions, but baby crocodiles need freshwater. Development along the coast of the Everglades and in the Keys has also caused loss of habitat. Scientists think it is unlikely that crocodiles will be able to survive outside the protected environment of the national parks in the future.

The Florida panther is a large, brown cat with a long tail. Panthers require a large area for hunting, but their hunting ground has been greatly reduced over the years. Many forests in the Everglades have been cleared so that the land can be used for farming and building homes. Panthers have been killed by hunters and by highway accidents. Some also die of mercury poisoning, which they get from eating animals that live in water polluted with mercury. In 1986, scientists put radio collars on panthers to track their living patterns, including their hunting ranges and their choices of habitats. It is believed that by 1990, there were only between 30 and 50 Florida panthers remaining. Those numbers have remained about the same to this day.

Man-made canals and dams designed to control the water flow in the Everglades have resulted in too much or too little water reaching the natural habitats of many animals. When there is too little water, many of the animals that panthers depend on for food move to other habitats. This pie chart shows that over 88% of a panther's diet consists of white-tailed deer, wild hogs, raccoons, and armadillos.

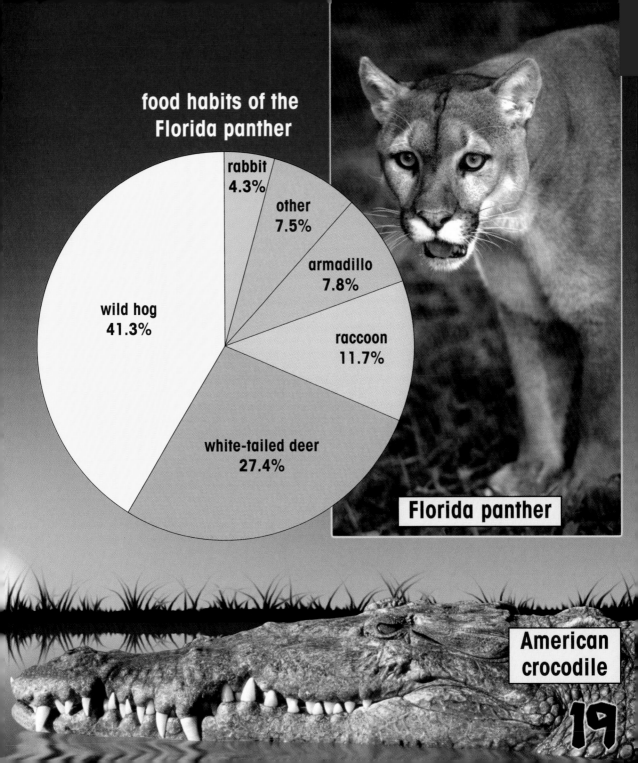

food habits of the Florida panther

- rabbit 4.3%
- other 7.5%
- armadillo 7.8%
- raccoon 11.7%
- wild hog 41.3%
- white-tailed deer 27.4%

Florida panther

American crocodile

The manatee, or sea cow, is a very large mammal that can grow to between 8 and 15 feet in length and weigh up to 1,000 pounds. Manatees are gentle animals and have very few enemies. They live in slow-moving, shallow estuaries and saltwater bays. The manatee's survival has been threatened mostly by people. As the population of Florida grows and nearby cities expand, manatees lose more of their natural habitat. Manatees are often injured or killed by boats. Everglades National Park has marked many areas with signs to alert boaters to slow down and watch for manatees.

Researchers and scientists are also working on ways to preserve the habitats of threatened animals in the Everglades. The American alligator, found in freshwater marshes, was once listed as an endangered animal in the Everglades. Although their population has recovered, they are still on the threatened list. The biggest problem for alligators is the water-control system that is used to release water into the park. If the water is released into the park in late June, before the alligator eggs are hatched, the nests get flooded and the eggs drown. Alligators are very important to the survival of many habitats in the Everglades because the holes they dig supply water for a variety of animals during the dry season.

manatee

animal group	species	threatened	endangered
birds	Arctic peregrine falcon	X	
	Cape Sable seaside sparrow		X
	piping plover	X	
	red-cockaded woodpecker		X
	roseate tern	X	
	snail (Everglade) kite		X
	southern bald eagle	X	
	wood stork		X
insects	Schaus swallowtail butterfly		X
invertebrates	Stock Island tree snail	X	
mammals	Florida panther		X
	Key Largo cotton mouse		X
	Key Largo woodrat		X
	West Indian manatee		X
reptiles	American alligator	X	
	American crocodile		X
	Atlantic ridley turtle		X
	Eastern indigo snake	X	
	green turtle		X
	leatherback turtle		X
	loggerhead turtle	X	

This table lists some of the threatened and endangered animals that live in the Everglades. How many animals from each group are endangered?

21

Plants of the Everglades

The Everglades ecosystem provides natural habitats for many colorful bromeliads, 25 varieties of orchids, 1,000 kinds of seed-bearing plants, and 120 kinds of trees. People who study plants come to the Everglades to learn about the unique way that temperate and tropical plants live side by side in this ecosystem. Tropical trees such as the gumbo limbo and mahogany grow alongside willows, pines, and oaks. Epiphytes such as the wild orchid grow on other plants and get all the water and **nutrients** they need from the air. An orchid called the night-blooming epidendrum (eh-puh-DEHN-druhm) grows in all of the park's habitats. This plant has white blossoms and is believed by many to be the most beautiful and fragrant orchid in the park.

There are more than 100 types of marsh plants in the Everglades. The most well-known is saw grass, which has created thousands of acres of marshland. Floating water plants include white water lilies, bladderwort, and maidencane. Algae floats on or just below the water's surface throughout the Everglades. Just as it is important to protect the wildlife of the Everglades, it is also important to protect the natural beauty of the rare and unusual plants that grow there. Fire, the loss of habitat, and the illegal removal of plants have caused some Everglades plants to become endangered. Others have become extinct.

The table at the top of page 23 shows some of the plants of the Everglades that are on the threatened and endangered list. How many plants on this list are endangered? How many on this list are threatened?

threatened and endangered
plants of the Everglades

species	threatened	endangered
Ashe's savory (lavender basil)	X	
Christmas berry		X
dwarf epidendrum		X
Fuch's bromeliad		X
Garber's spurge		X
green violet		X
moss orchid		X
pine pink orchid	X	
rain lily	X	
southern lady fern	X	
sweetshrub	X	
yellow hibiscus		X

water lilies

Everglades Preservation

The Everglades has been identified as one of the nation's most threatened ecosystems. This area has been reduced to half of its original size due to farming, the growth of nearby cities, and water-management systems used to control the flow of water in and out of the Everglades.

Over the years, people have altered the natural water cycles of the Everglades. In the 1900s, settlers drained and cleared parts of the Everglades for farming. In the late 1940s, floodwalls and canals were built to drain water from the Everglades and send it to nearby cities with growing populations. These developments permanently changed the water flow in the Everglades. Over time, such practices, as well as pollution from farms and cities, have led to a severe loss of food and habitat for many animals in this area. As a result, many of the animals that live in the Everglades have become endangered. Scientists believe that if something isn't done to reverse the effects the water-management systems have had on southern Florida, many of these endangered animals will become extinct.

Today, the canal system consists of 1,400 miles of canals, which drain water from most of the shallow rivers of the Everglades. A dam holds back the water from Lake Okeechobee, which used to flow directly into the park. Some of the water is channeled to farmlands south of the lake where thousands of acres of sugarcane are grown. The remaining water is drained into 1 of 3 Everglades conservation areas. Occasionally, some of this water is released into Everglades National Park.

demand for water in Lake Okeechobee area

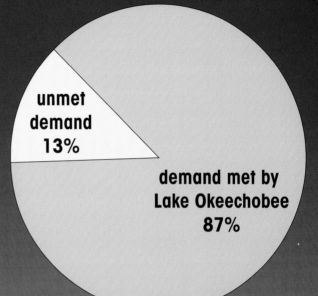

unmet demand 13%

demand met by Lake Okeechobee 87%

For many years, water-control systems have taken water out of Lake Okeechobee and redirected it to nearby farming areas and cities. This pie chart shows how much of the demand for water has been met by Lake Okeechobee and how much goes unmet due to a lack of water.

canals at edge of Lake Okeechobee

Due to the difficulty of monitoring exactly how much water is released into Everglades National Park, some areas may get too much or too little water. When too much water is let in during the dry season, flooding occurs and many animals have difficulty finding food. When not enough water is allowed in, many animals may have to leave their natural habitats to survive. Both of these conditions can cause a dangerous decrease in the wildlife population of the Everglades. Scientists are trying to find ways of restoring the water-flow patterns that existed hundreds of years ago in the original Everglades. This will allow water to flow across the land and into the Gulf of Mexico naturally, as was the case before the water flow was altered.

Scientists are also concerned about water containing chemicals from fertilizers being released into the Everglades. These chemicals harm some of the plants that grow here and affect the food chains that much of the wildlife depends upon, in turn affecting the health and natural habitats of animals.

This process creates another problem that continues to threaten the delicate ecosystem of the Everglades—the need for clean water. Without freshwater, many of the animals in the Everglades would not be able to survive. Scientists believe that water conservation and better management of water distribution to the Everglades and surrounding cities may help solve this problem.

This map of southern Florida shows the direction of water flow from Lake Okeechobee to the Gulf of Mexico prior to the time that modern water-management systems were constructed. Use the map key, which is a type of table, to read and understand the map.

historic water
flow patterns

key

	Everglades National Park
	water flow

27

The National Park Service and other government agencies continue to research and develop plans that provide solutions to the water-management problems and loss of wildlife in the Everglades. One step to making these changes is to pass laws that help protect and preserve the Everglades. In 1989, former President George Bush signed the Everglades National Park and Protection Act into law. This bill approved the addition of 109,000 acres of the east Everglades to the park. It also stated that parts of the canal system should be taken apart to restore the natural water flow of the Kissimmee River and the surrounding waters. This legislation was created to protect the plants and animals, as well as the drinking water.

The Comprehensive Everglades Restoration Plan (CERP) passed by Congress in 2000 is the largest environmental restoration project ever proposed in the United States. The CERP is a proposal to restore, protect, and preserve the water resources of central and southern Florida, including the Everglades, at an estimated cost of $8 billion. The plan was designed to hold back, store, and redistribute freshwater as well as monitor the amount of freshwater that is used in this area. The plan addresses some issues specific to the Everglades, including improved water flow to the Everglades and its estuaries, treatment of the wetlands, and improved management of the water coming from Lake Okeechobee. It is estimated that this plan will take more than 30 years to complete.

Under the current water-management system, 1.7 billion gallons of water that once flowed through the Everglades each day is now dumped into the Atlantic Ocean and the Gulf of Mexico. Some of the proposals made by the Comprehensive Everglades Restoration Plan are to restore the amount and quality of water that the Everglades needs to maintain an ecological balance and to provide freshwater to populated areas.

current
flow

key

	Everglades National Park
	water flow

proposed
flow

The efforts of scientists, researchers, and government officials can make a difference in preserving the Everglades ecosystem. However, the changes that take place also depend on each of us supporting conservation laws and protecting the environment in our own way every day. We must work to protect natural environments like the Everglades to make sure they survive in the years to come. Even if you do not live near the Everglades, there are things you can do to help protect all natural environments:

- Find out which plants and animals in your state are threatened or endangered, and learn how you can help protect them.

- Check to make sure that you are not buying products made from endangered plants or wildlife.

- Support conservation laws.

- Conserve water whenever possible.

The charts, graphs, and tables in this book help to show that the plants and animals of the Everglades are closely connected, and that they depend on one another for survival. The delicate balance of this ecosystem must be carefully maintained in order for natural habitats to survive. There is still a chance of saving Everglades National Park as long as we continue to support the research and laws that protect one of our most beautiful natural environments.

bromeliad (broh-MEE-lee-ad) A tropical air plant that grows on trees.

ecosystem (EE-koh-sis-tuhm) The whole group of living and nonliving things that make up an environment and affect each other.

endangered (in-DAYN-juhrd) In danger of becoming extinct.

environment (en-VY-uhrn-ment) All the surrounding things, conditions, and influences affecting the growth of living things.

epiphyte (EH-puh-fyt) Any plant that grows on another plant but does not use this plant for food. Epiphytes get their food and nutrients from the air.

estuary (ESS-chuh-wear-ee) A water passage where a saltwater tide meets a freshwater river current.

habitat (HA-buh-tat) The place where a plant or animal grows or lives.

invertebrate (in-VUHR-tuh-bruht) An animal that has no backbone.

nutrient (NU-tree-uhnt) Any substance needed by living things for energy, growth, and repair of tissues.

preserve (prih-ZUHRV) An area set aside for the protection of animals.

saw grass (SAW GRASS) A type of sedge that covers large marsh areas in the Everglades.

sedge (SEHJ) A plant that is like grass but has solid stems and grows in marshes.

subtropical (suhb-TRAH-puh-kuhl) Areas bordering on the tropical zone.

temperate (TEM-puh-raht) A climate that is not too hot or too cold.

threatened (THREH-tehnd) Likely to become endangered.